Disney's

TALES from AGRABAH

Seven Original Stories of Aladdin and Jasmine

by Katherine Applegate
illustrated by
Fred Marvin and José Cardona

DISNEY PRESS

NEW YORK

For Stu, Martha, and Lisa, with love

FIRST EDITION
1 3 5 7 9 10 8 6 4 2
Library of Congress Catalog Card Number: 94-71484
ISBN: 0-7868-3023-9

CONTENTS

A Gift from the Stars

Princess Jasmine stared out her window into the deep of the desert night. The sands seemed to spill out to the end of the world like a rolling black sea, but it was the sky that held her gaze.

"Jasmine?" She heard a gentle knock at her bedchamber door. The Sultan peeked in. "Dearest, I heard you walking around in here. Can't you sleep?"

Jasmine shook her head. In the moonlight her dark eyes shone with unshed tears.

The Sultan guessed what his daughter was thinking about. "I miss her, too, dearest," he said softly. He joined her on the window seat. "Do you remember that story your mother used to tell you when you couldn't sleep?" He stroked his beard. "About a tiger cub, wasn't it?"

"Rajah." Jasmine managed a small smile. "The star tiger. You can see him if you try, Father." She pointed toward the sky. "See that tiny yellow star? That's his eye blinking at us."

The Sultan cocked his head one way, then the other. But it

was like staring at one of his toy puzzles for too long. None of the pieces fell into place.

"Do you see him, Father?"

"Well, I believe *you* see him, and that's quite good enough for me."

"It takes practice," Jasmine told him. "But Mama could always find Rajah."

The Sultan's shoulders slumped. What kind of father was he that he couldn't find a tiger in the stars? He wasn't fit to raise a daughter like Jasmine alone, one so full of energy and imagination.

"Would you tell me Mama's Rajah story, Father?"

"Well, now. Let me see. Rajah is a tiger cub, that much I remember." The Sultan hesitated. He was not a very good storyteller. He often lost his way and had to start over.

"A tiger cub who lives in the *sky*," Jasmine added.

"Yes, yes, a star tiger," said the Sultan. "And he has a big fluffy mane, and—"

"No, Father." Jasmine shook her head and yawned. "That's a *lion*. Rajah is a tiger. Each night after I go to sleep, Rajah climbs down out of the sky to guard me."

"He comes right here to the palace, eh?"

"Well, mostly to my room, since he's my tiger." Jasmine yawned again and closed her eyes. "He stays all night so I won't be afraid of the dark."

"Jasmine?" the Sultan whispered, but she was already fast asleep. He carried her to her bed and gently covered her with a blanket. Tiptoeing back to the window, the Sultan tried to catch one last glimpse of Rajah, but the little cub was lost in a fiery jungle of stars.

Halfway through the night, Jasmine suddenly awoke. From

across the room came a noise—a low, throaty hum, like honeybees in a deep well.

Alarmed, Jasmine sat up and stared into the darkness. Two yellow eyes gazed back at her, glimmering like new gold coins floating in midair. Behind the eyes she could just make out a white muzzle and a furry little gold-and-black-striped body.

"Rajah?" she whispered in disbelief.

The eyes blinked. Jasmine cautiously climbed out of bed and crept closer until she could gently reach out and touch the tiger cub.

"How did you get here, little Rajah?" she whispered.

Clumsily the cub leaped into her arms, a bundle of warm silken fur. He was a mere kitten, but Jasmine could see hints of the powerful animal he would someday grow to be.

Jasmine carried Rajah to her bed. He snuggled beside her, and she covered him with her blanket. Hugging him close, lulled by his contented purr, she fell back into a deep, dreamless sleep.

The next morning when Jasmine awoke, Rajah was still beside her. He was lying on his back, all four big paws in the air, snoring softly. It hadn't been a dream—he was real.

Rajah opened his eyes and leaped to his feet. He licked Jasmine's face until she couldn't stop giggling. "Be serious, now," she said firmly. "I have to think quickly." Rajah was too busy pouncing on her toes to listen, but she continued. "You're just a tiny kitten now, but you're going to grow up to be an awfully big tiger. And I'm afraid Father would never allow a tiger to roam the palace. At least, I don't think he would." Rajah growled at his newly discovered tail. "Maybe you could stay here in my room," Jasmine said, staring at him thoughtfully. "But no. The palace staff would find you. What I need is a secret place for you to hide during the day. But don't worry, it's just until I can find a sure way to convince Father to let you stay."

Jasmine jumped out of bed and dressed quickly. She placed Rajah in a wicker basket and piled clothes around the cub, who promptly began chewing on a silk veil. "Now behave, Rajah," she cautioned. "We're going on a little trip."

Jasmine fastened the lid on the basket and slipped down the hall. She knew just the place to hide the cub—a musty unused storage room in a far corner of the palace.

As Jasmine stole through the lush palace gardens, she was surprised to see guards racing back and forth through the shrubs, their swords drawn. The Sultan was standing in the center of the gardens near a large fountain, nervously pacing to and fro.

"Jasmine, dearest!" cried the Sultan before his daughter could

dart behind a bush. "I just sent one of the guards to check on you. Such excitement! It seems they've found actual tiger tracks right here in the gardens. They say it's a small tiger—but where there's one, there could be more."

"Imagine that," said Jasmine weakly as Rajah tried to poke his nose out of the basket.

"Sultan!" a woman's voice screeched. "Is it safe yet?"

"Who was that?" Jasmine asked.

"Syreeta. One of my subjects. She invited herself over for brunch," said the Sultan with a little sigh. He led Jasmine past a tall hedge. Atop a marble lion sculpture sat a portly woman, clinging to it for dear life. Perched on her head was a little monkey wearing a fancy embroidered vest and fez.

"I assure you, everything's quite under control," Jafar, the Sultan's royal vizier, was calling to the woman.

"Under control!" squawked Jafar's pet parrot, Iago, from his usual spot on his master's shoulder.

"Come down from there, Syreeta! Why, it's just a baby tiger," said the Sultan. "At least, we *think* it is. It must have escaped from the traveling menagerie that left town yesterday. Now, if it were one of those full-grown, slobbering man-eating tigers—" He shuddered, his face turning pale at the thought.

"I'm quite happy up here," said Syreeta. She nodded at Jasmine. "You must be the princess. Charmed. Meet my monkey, Abu."

In the blink of an eye the little monkey leaped down onto Jasmine's basket and began tugging at the top to see what was inside.

"Behave now, monkey-poo!" Syreeta chided from her perch.

"Monkey-poo!" screeched Iago.

"Well, I'll keep an eye out for that tiger," Jasmine said. Keeping a firm grip on the basket lid, she tried to shoo away Syreeta's nosy monkey.

"What's in the basket, Jasmine?" Jafar asked suddenly, eyes narrowed.

"Basket? What—oh, you mean *this* basket. Um, laundry! Dirty laundry."

"But dearest, we have servants to take care of that," said the Sultan distractedly, still looking around for the escaped tiger.

"You know me," Jasmine said quickly. "I love to help out." From inside the basket Rajah let out a kittenish growl. "Breakfast time!" Jasmine chirped, rubbing her stomach. She grabbed Abu and deposited him on Jafar's free shoulder, then scurried off across the garden.

"Monkey-poo!" Iago taunted. Abu, annoyed, jumped on Jafar's head and sprang at Iago, managing to snare a handful of feathers.

"Lovely child," said Syreeta from her perch.

"Yes," Jafar muttered, dumping both bird and monkey off his shoulders onto the ground. "And so helpful."

To Jasmine's relief, as the days passed, the furor over the tiger tracks died down. She and Rajah often prowled the nighttime palace together. The tiger cub spent many happy hours terrorizing the palace mice and chasing fireflies in the garden. He also took great delight in teething on the soft leather of Jafar's favorite shoes. And when he grew tired he would curl up in Jasmine's lap while she combed his soft fur with her silver comb and sang old lullabies her mother had taught her.

Each morning, as the sun peeked over the farthest dune on the horizon, Jasmine brought Rajah back to his daytime hideaway. She tried to make it as cozy as possible, with balls of yarn to chase and a silk pillow by the sunniest window. And at noon she always made sure to sneak him a plate of delicious food from the kitchen.

Still, Jasmine wished more than anything that she could tell her father about Rajah. She had never kept a secret from him before, and part of her was sure that her father would love the baby tiger as much as she did. But another part of her realized that Rajah would soon grow up into a large adult tiger—and she still wasn't so sure her father would approve of such a pet, especially after what he'd said in the gardens. She just couldn't take any chances.

One morning Jasmine awoke to a palace abuzz with activity. Prince Mahmud, a dear friend of the Sultan's who ruled a splendid city far across the desert, was coming to visit with his whole entourage.

Jasmine was thrilled when the guests began to arrive. She

loved meeting new people, especially when they came from far-off lands. The prince brought her a wonderful flute carved of the rarest wood. He taught her how to play a few notes, and before long Jasmine was entertaining the guests with a simple tune. She was having so much fun that she forgot all about Rajah's noontime meal.

As a matter of fact, she forgot about Rajah altogether.

The first evening stars were already appearing when Jasmine remembered her friend. She dropped her flute and ran to the secret hideaway as fast as her legs would carry her.

"Rajah!" she cried breathlessly as she threw open the door. "I'm so sorry—"

Her heart dropped. Rajah was gone!

She ran to the open window. Beneath the sill, a palm swayed gently in the evening breeze. But there was no sign of the little cub.

Frantically Jasmine searched every nook and cranny of the palace, racing past her father's guests, tearing through the menagerie, plunging into the busy kitchen.

"Where *is* that goat's milk?" cried Safiya, the Sultan's head cook, as Jasmine dashed through. "It was here a minute ago." She frowned. "Jasmine! What on earth—"

"Have you seen—," Jasmine began, but then she stopped. What could she say? *Have you seen my secret tiger?*

"Be off now, dear," Safiya said. "You should be getting dressed. The banquet will be starting soon."

With a heavy heart, Jasmine went to her bedchamber and changed into her golden robes. Rajah was gone; it was that simple. And it was all her fault. She'd left him, forgotten and alone, in a dismal, cramped little room. Who could blame him for leaving?

* * *

12

The banquet that evening was an opulent affair. At the huge dining table princes and noblemen sat, dressed in glittering finery. The table overflowed with platters of delicious food. Glasses clinked and laughter filled the air while musicians played merrily.

But Jasmine was not feeling merry. She stared into her silver soup bowl, not eating a bite.

"Are you all right, Jasmine?" the Sultan whispered as the servants cleared the table for the main course. "You look like you're a million leagues away."

Jasmine hesitated. How could she tell her father what had happened? She had kept the truth from him for so long. "I'm just a little tired," she said quietly at last.

The Sultan nodded sympathetically, then turned to Prince Mahmud. "Wait until you try Safiya's specialty," he said enthusiastically as servants positioned a heavy silver tray with a round cover on the table. "It's an old family recipe."

"You can't imagine how hungry I am," said the prince as one of the servants reached for the cover. "Why, I could eat a—"

Suddenly the room fell as silent as a desert night.

There, lying on his back, big paws splayed in the air, was Rajah. His white stomach bulged like a furry mountain. He licked his chops, then let out an earsplitting burp.

"Run!" the prince screamed. "Run for your lives!"

Chairs and dishes flew as the guests ran pell-mell for the door. Only Safiya, the Sultan, and Jasmine stayed behind. "Father," said Jasmine as she grabbed Rajah and hugged him to her tightly. "There's someone I'd like you to meet—"

"My roast!" Safiya moaned. "He ate my entire roast!"

"Nice kitty-kitty," said the Sultan with a nervous gulp. "I hope he left me some dessert."

That night Jasmine curled up in bed with Rajah, waiting for the Sultan to tuck them in. "Whatever happens, no more hiding,

Rajah," she whispered. "You're free to come and go as you please."

The Sultan came in and perched on the edge of Jasmine's bed, giving Rajah a tentative pat on the head. "Jasmine," he said with a sigh. "I know you've grown attached to Rajah, but I'm sure you realize he can't stay."

"But Father—"

"He'd disrupt the whole palace—why, look at what happened at the banquet!" Rajah yawned. "And those teeth!" the Sultan added. "Imagine when he's full grown! Suppose someday we have a visitor he doesn't like. One good munch and—" The Sultan shuddered. "For that matter, what if he decides he doesn't like *me*?"

Rajah leaped up and licked the Sultan's nose. The Sultan was so startled that he nearly fell off the bed.

"But he *does* like you, see?" Jasmine said.

"Well, er, yes," the Sultan said, dabbing at his nose with a corner of his robe. "That may be. But the other problem is, we know that his rightful owner is looking for him. After all, he must be the tiger that escaped from the traveling menagerie."

"I know where he came from," Jasmine said. "Mama sent him. *I'm* his rightful owner." She gazed at her father earnestly. "You don't believe me, do you?"

"I believe that you believe, dearest. But he still can't stay, don't you see that?"

"*You're* the one who doesn't see," Jasmine whispered.

With a sigh, the Sultan kissed Jasmine's forehead. She closed her eyes and turned away.

The Sultan returned to his throne room. Jabbar, the owner of the traveling menagerie, had arrived and was waiting for him.

"Ah, Jabbar," the Sultan said. "I was expecting you." He sank onto his throne and stared at Jabbar for a long time, lost in thought. As a rule he tried to avoid thinking so hard. It gave him indigestion.

"It seems, Jabbar, that I have a dilemma on my hands," the Sultan said at last. "Perhaps you can help me solve it."

"I will do my best to be of service, Your Majesty," Jabbar replied with a bow. "What do you wish of me?"

"We did find the tiger cub you lost," the Sultan said. "But it seems my daughter has become quite attached to the beast. I wonder if you would accept this gold in exchange for him?" He pulled a pouch from his pocket and held it out.

Jabbar took the pouch, smiling as he felt its weight. "It seems a more than generous exchange to me, Your Highness," he said, bowing again. "I wish you and your daughter long lives and happiness." Still bowing and smiling, he backed out of the room.

When Jabbar was gone, the Sultan returned to Jasmine's room to check on her. She was fast asleep, Rajah cradled in her arms.

The Sultan smiled down at them fondly. He could get used to Rajah, he thought. He paused at Jasmine's window. It was a clear night, and the stars were shining brightly. He watched them for a moment. But as he turned to leave, he hesitated. Something was wrong. He couldn't quite put his finger on it, but he had the craziest feeling that a piece of the starry sky was missing.

Monkeying Around

"Abu! Abitty-bu! Where are you hiding, my little monkey-poo?"

Abu jerked up, slamming his head on the top of his owner's glittering jewel box. Syreeta! Drat! He cast one last admiring glance at his reflection in the mirror. With Syreeta's ruby earring hanging from his ear, he looked every bit the roguish pirate.

"Fuzzy-feet! Amaris and Shatara are here, and we have a surprise for you!"

Abu somersaulted onto the bed and dove deep into the safety of a silk pillowcase.

"Funny, I could have sworn he'd be in here," Syreeta said to her friends. "He sleeps most of the day, you know. Lazy, useless animals, monkeys. Between you and me, Abu is getting rather tiresome. But I do think wearing him gives me a certain style, don't you?"

She dropped down heavily onto her bed. With a screech, Abu popped out of the pillowcase.

"There you are, you little fiend! And you've been in my jewels

again!" Syreeta yanked her earring off Abu's ear and grabbed him by the tail. "Look what I had Nassir the tailor stitch up."

Amaris held up a frilly pink clown costume. Shatara displayed a pair of tiny, floppy shoes and a pom-pom-topped pointy hat. They were small enough for a baby to wear. Or even a . . . uh-oh. Abu gulped.

"You are going to look adorable, snuggle-tail," Syreeta announced triumphantly. "And when *you* look adorable, *I* look adorable."

Abu gazed at the outfit in horror. He'd suffered many indignities at Syreeta's hands, but this—this was unthinkable! For one thing, pink was just not his color.

"It will match my own outfit perfectly," Syreeta continued. "The Sultan's having a costume party next week at the palace. With you sitting on my shoulder, we'll be the talk of Agrabah."

The palace! Abu gazed longingly out the window at the golden domes gleaming in the distance. The time had come to move on, and Abu knew just where he belonged—the palace. He'd escorted Syreeta on a visit to the Sultan just the other day and seen how well the palace pets lived. None of them had to dance on command or wear tacky costumes. If Iago, that crackers-for-brains parrot, could live there, why not Abu?

Abu yanked his tail free and made a wild dash toward the window. "Abu, you . . . you furry ingrate!" Syreeta cried, but it was too late. He was already doing a nice back-flip-somersault combination onto the palm tree outside the window. Unfortunately, thanks to his weakness for sugared dates, he was a little out of shape. The branch snapped, and he landed in a pile of camel dung. He brushed off his vest and gave Syreeta a jaunty wave. He was a free monkey at last. Dirty, but free. He scurried off toward the gleaming palace, soon leaving Syreeta's angry shouts far behind him.

By the time he reached the center of Agrabah sometime later, Abu was parched and weary. The marketplace was a teeming mass of strange sights and smells. Rich and poor mingled together, merchants and noblemen, waifs and stray dogs. Abu's refined nose was assaulted by the most unappetizing smells, his sensitive ears assailed by all manner of undignified shouts.

Abu gazed longingly at the palace beckoning in the distance. It appeared to be a mere peanut's throw away, but he'd already discovered that distances could be deceiving when you were using your own four feet. Spying a cart piled high with ripe, tempting fruit, he decided to eat and rest before continuing. A juicy apple would hit the spot nicely.

Abu scampered up the fruit vendor's leg and perched on his shoulder. He chattered a hello and gave the man a big wet kiss on the cheek.

"You miserable fleabag!" the vendor cried, arms flailing. "Be off, or I'll have monkey stew for dinner!"

Abu was shocked. With Syreeta, a little begging always resulted in a mountain of food. How could this fruit seller fail to be enchanted by Abu's obvious charms?

Abu dangled from the top of the cart by his tail and batted his eyes. The vendor grabbed a stick and sliced the air, narrowly missing Abu's tail.

Fine. He could take a hint.

Abu tried again at the bread seller's stand. The old man flung a stale round of pita bread at him. The next vendor made a direct hit with a sack of lentil pilaf.

Feeling painfully hungry and embarrassingly disheveled, Abu rested next to a nut seller's stand, hoping a stray peanut or two might fall to the ground. A few minutes later a young boy in patched and tattered clothes approached the nut seller. "Fine-looking pistachios, Anwar," said the boy with a mischievous smile.

"Be off, street rat," said Anwar. "Or I'll have Rasoul on your tail."

The boy wandered off a few paces, loitering near the other side of the stand. After a few minutes Anwar turned his back to roast a fresh batch of peanuts.

Now was Abu's big chance. If the vendors wouldn't give him any food, he'd just have to help himself. He reached up stealthily and snatched a sack of pistachio nuts. To his surprise, the sack yanked back. "Let go!" someone hissed.

Abu peered over the top of the stand. The ragged little boy was on the other side, clutching the same sack. Abu tugged. The boy tugged back.

Anwar spun around and spied Abu. "Lousy vermin!" he cried.

Before Abu could run, the boy grabbed his arm and leaned close. He had a devilish glint in his eye. "I'll split it with you. Just play along," the boy whispered. When Abu hesitated, the boy added, "Come on. Do you trust me?"

Abu shrugged. What choice did he have?

The boy grabbed Abu and cradled the squirming monkey in his arms. "Is that really what you want your last meal to be, little guy?" He looked over at Anwar. "He isn't long for this world."

Anwar eyed Abu doubtfully. "Looks pretty healthy to me. Healthy enough to steal, the little bandit."

"That's how it is with the monkey pox," the boy said. "One minute you're pinching pistachios. The next—" The boy ran a finger across his throat.

Abu coughed and wheezed with great dramatic flair. Too much flair, perhaps, because the boy nudged him in the ribs.

"It's not . . . catching, is it?" Anwar asked nervously.

"No. That is, hardly ever. Only if you eat something he's touched, and hey, how likely is that?"

Anwar glanced down at the sack of nuts Abu still clutched. Abu let out a ferocious sneeze.

"Get rid of that vile creature!" Anwar cried. "And take that sack with you. Burn it, destroy it, just get it away!"

The boy didn't need to be told twice. He scurried off into the maze of shops and alleys, still clutching Abu and the bag. Before long he reached the roof of an abandoned building. "Nice job," he said to Abu, opening the bag. "We make a good team, you and I. By the way, the name's Aladdin."

They shared the nuts in silence. Abu ate hungrily, though not as hungrily as the boy. Still, Abu noticed that Aladdin left exactly half the nuts for him.

"You know," said Aladdin when they'd finished, "with you as a distraction, I could steal twice what I do." He walked to the edge of the crumbling roof and stared off into the distance. "Not that I *want* to steal," he said softly. "But hey, I gotta eat, right?" He turned around, eyeing Abu speculatively. "So where'd you come from, anyway? And where are you going?"

Abu shrugged expressively.

Aladdin grinned. "Well, it doesn't matter. Wherever you're from, you're welcome to stay here with me for a while, if you like."

Here? The boy actually lived *here*? Abu looked around. The rooftop was dirty and drafty and full of junk. It wasn't a fit residence even for a rat, and Abu had a very low opinion of rats. In fact, the only good thing about it was that it had a fine view of the palace. Abu hopped up onto a crumbling wall and stared at it.

"I mean, I could use the company," Aladdin said. "But I'd understand if you said no. This isn't exactly the palace. . . ." He noticed where Abu was looking. "Oh," he said. "So *that's* where you're going?"

Abu nodded enthusiastically. The palace was where he belonged, not here on a rooftop with this street rat—even if he did seem nice. Still, it wouldn't do to show up at the palace this dusty and unkempt. Tomorrow morning he'd get himself cleaned up and be on his way. Tonight he would stay here.

Together Aladdin and Abu sat on the edge of the roof, watching the moon turn the desert sands into a rippled silver sea. Aladdin reached for a crude wooden flute and began to play. It was a lovely song, sprightly and wistful at the same time, and Abu found himself twitching his tail to the rhythm. Before he knew it he was dancing across the rooftop, bouncing and spinning and chasing his tail. Aladdin laughed and applauded, and suddenly Abu realized it was the first time he'd ever danced on his own—not for Syreeta or her friends but for the sheer, silly joy of it.

"Morning! Ready to go borrow some breakfast?"

Abu blinked and yawned, adjusting the kink in his tail. What a mess he was! He was in desperate need of a bubble bath and a good manicure.

"How about a coconut to start things off?" Aladdin asked, hoisting Abu up onto his shoulder.

Abu hesitated. He really should be heading off to the palace. But it was always a good idea to start off the day with a hearty breakfast. First the coconut, then the palace.

"Shall we try the monkey pox routine again?" Aladdin asked as they headed into the busy marketplace. "Or how about—" He stopped in midsentence. Nailed to a palm tree was a large, official-looking notice.

"Hmm," said Aladdin as he read. "So *that's* your story."

Story? Abu squinted at the human scribblings. Suddenly Aladdin spun around, heading down the street. Abu tugged on Aladdin's ear and pointed at the fruit stand back in the market-place, chattering hungrily.

Aladdin grabbed Abu's tail and held on tight. "I know, Abu. But you'll be eating like a prince soon enough. And so will I. Twenty gold pieces! I've never even *seen* that much money!"

Abu? How had Aladdin figured out his name?

"See, the thing is," Aladdin continued, "you're obviously a classy monkey. Pampered. Not street-smart like me. You could starve out here." He seemed to be trying to convince himself of something. "Sure, that reward will buy me a lot of good meals, but the more important thing is that I do what's right for you."

Reward? So that was it. Syreeta had put up a sign about Abu's escape, offering a reward for his return. So much for

trusting this street rat! Abu's heart sank. The worst part was that he'd actually been thinking he'd miss Aladdin a little when he left for the palace.

Abu squirmed and screeched and carried on, twisting and writhing, but Aladdin hung on firmly, and before long they reached Syreeta's magnificent house. Aladdin gaped at the impressive marble entryway. "You lived *here* and you actually ran away? You must be crazy."

A servant opened the door a crack. "No beggars," he said coldly.

Aladdin stuck his foot in the door. "Wait! I've found your monkey."

"Abu!" cried a large woman, dashing to the door. "Syreeta's little Abitty-bu!" She grabbed Abu and smothered him in kisses. "Come here, monkey-poo! You furry little demon, you."

Aladdin felt a twinge of jealousy. What he wouldn't give to be welcomed into a home this magnificent—even if it did mean getting buried in sloppy kisses. And yet, strangely, Abu looked so trapped, squirming unhappily in Syreeta's arms.

"About that . . . reward?" Aladdin reminded her. He had to look away as Abu's pleading eyes met his.

"Oh yes, the reward," Syreeta said, struggling to maintain her hold on Abu. She led Aladdin inside and summoned a servant, who soon returned with a small sack of gold.

Aladdin peeked inside and smiled. With all this money, he thought, I can eat for weeks, months, maybe even years! And not just day-old pita, either. "Well," he said, hefting the bag over his shoulder, "I guess I'll be going." He looked at Abu. "Don't run away again, little guy. You've got it made here. Trust me."

"Oh, he won't be running away again," said Syreeta. "I've made sure of that."

Aladdin turned. "Really?"

"Yes indeed. I had a lovely cage specially made to match the furniture in the parlor. Double locked. Even this nasty little wizard won't escape." She pointed across the room to a tall golden cage. Suspended inside was a tiny swing.

Abu shrieked and clawed as she carried him over, but Syreeta shoved him inside the cage and slammed the door. "Try to escape now!" she said. "You've cost me enough, you little monster. You'll be lucky if I even wear you to the Sultan's party. I'm thinking of getting a parrot instead, like the lovely one that Jafar fellow has. Of course, I'll have to reconsider my entire outfit. . . ."

As the woman continued to talk, Abu extended his paw through the golden bars, beckoning to Aladdin. He gave a soft, miserable moan.

The sack of coins felt heavy in Aladdin's hand. "Well," he said, clearing his throat. "I guess I'll be going." He nodded good-bye to Abu, not meeting the little monkey's pleading gaze.

Aladdin headed for the door. The bag of coins jingled softly. What delicacy should he buy first? With all this money, he could have anything he wanted. Although right at the moment he seemed to have lost his appetite.

Suddenly Aladdin spun around. "One last hug good-bye," he said, rushing back to the parlor.

Syreeta looked surprised. "Well, all right," she said reluctantly.

Aladdin leaned into the cage, the sack still slung over his back. Abu backed away from Aladdin, eyes narrowed. "Come here, my little fuzzy-buns," Aladdin cooed. Then in a low whisper he added, "Do you trust me?"

Abu hesitated for a moment. "Come on, little guy," Aladdin urged softly. "What do you have to lose? If you stay here, you're trapped forever."

While Syreeta watched, the monkey rushed into Aladdin's outstretched arms. Aladdin took a deep breath. "Hang on tight!" he whispered.

With Abu clinging to his shoulder, he turned and raced toward the door.

"Stop! Monkey thief!" Syreeta screamed when she realized what was happening.

Aladdin dodged around her, but two servants were blocking the door, and more were racing up behind him. He needed to distract them. He glanced at the sack he was still carrying, then at Abu. "Oh well," Aladdin said. "I guess it's back to stealing to eat."

He opened the sack and scattered the gold pieces all over the floor. They poured out in a glittering stream, and just for a second Aladdin hesitated. All that money! Then Abu chattered anxiously in his ear, and Aladdin swung into action. He jumped nimbly around the guards at the door, who were watching as the other servants slipped and slid on the gold coins. Before they could make a move to stop him, Aladdin had bolted out into the crowded streets. Abu held on tight, not looking back.

"Fine!" Syreeta screeched from behind them. "Keep the little ingrate! I hope you both starve, you pair of street rats!"

Aladdin didn't slow down until they had reached the safety of the bustling marketplace. "A guy *could* starve out here all alone, you know," he told Abu. While the owner's back was turned, Aladdin reached out and grabbed a couple of apples off a stand, so fast that Abu hardly saw it. "Life on the streets is tough." He shrugged and handed one of the apples to Abu. "I guess I'll head home now and eat. I suppose you'll be leaving for the palace. Who could blame you?"

Abu leaped down off Aladdin's shoulder.

"Of course," Aladdin added shyly, "if you wanted to stay with me . . ." He shrugged. "But no. Better for you to go to the palace. See you, little buddy."

Abu looked up. In the distance the palace beckoned enticingly. He could practically see the glittering jewels adorning his newly tailored clothes. He could practically taste the delicacies prepared by the Sultan's personal cook. He could practically smell the exotic flowers perfuming the menagerie.

Oh well. Perhaps someday Abu would make it to the palace. But for now he thought he'd stay in the marketplace with Aladdin—his first real friend.

He reached for Aladdin's hand. They were almost home, and Abu felt like dancing.

It's a Small World After All

"Oh, Sultan," Syreeta said as she swished into the throne room, "have you outgrown your royal robes again?" The Sultan stood on a stool while Nassir the tailor measured him.

"Too many lentil patties," said the Sultan, patting his round stomach and blushing a little.

"Too many poppy-seed cakes and fig pies," Iago whispered into Jafar's ear.

"I'm glad you're here, Syreeta," said the Sultan. "I need advice about my daughter."

Just then something furry jumped from Syreeta's arms onto her shoulder. The Sultan was so startled he nearly fell off his stool.

"Don't be frightened, Your Royalness!" Syreeta said. "This is my new pet ferret, Sami." She gave the ferret a sloppy kiss.

"I just lost my appetite," Iago muttered to Jafar.

"So what kind of advice do you need, Sultan?" Syreeta asked.

"Jasmine's birthday is coming in a few weeks, and I want to give her something special. Something perfect. Something for the girl who has everything."

"Perhaps she would like a ferret," said Syreeta. "They're very clean and only bite when you dress them up."

"Oh, Syreeta, you and your pets. Before the ferret it was a baby camel. Let's see, before that it was a parrot, wasn't it? And before him was that impudent little monkey," said the Sultan, chuckling. "Besides, Jasmine has Rajah."

"Perhaps the princess would like a new wardrobe," Nassir suggested. "I have a new shipment of the finest silk. Like spun gold, and so reasonably priced—"

The Sultan looked down at the tailor and sighed. "But Jasmine has all the clothes she could possibly want," he said. "And anyway, those things don't concern her much."

Nassir frowned. "Ouch!" said the Sultan. "You pinned me!"

"Sorry. My mistake." Nassir grinned.

"Perhaps, my lord," Jafar spoke up, "I could offer some assistance in this matter."

"Jafar," said the Sultan, "you *are* my royal adviser. So advise me."

"Might I suggest," said Jafar, "that etiquette lessons would be in order? Jasmine's such a . . . well, a high-spirited girl. It might do her good."

"The little brat," Iago muttered.

"What did he say?" asked the Sultan.

"Meaningless mutterings," Jafar said smoothly. Iago gave him a dirty look.

"In any case, I don't think etiquette lessons are for Jasmine," the Sultan said. "To begin with, she wouldn't go. And besides, I like her just the way she is."

"The other day," said Jafar, clearing his throat, "she hid a salamander in my turban. Hardly princesslike behavior, my lord."

"I'm tired of standing still," said the Sultan, ignoring Jafar. "And none of you has been very helpful." He climbed down off his stool. "I'm going to see Jasmine. Maybe if I drop the right hints, she'll tell me what she wants."

A few minutes later the Sultan found Jasmine in the library with her tutor, Aziza, a white-haired woman with a gentle smile. "Father," Jasmine cried when he entered. "Look what Aziza was showing me."

The Sultan peered over his daughter's shoulder. "It's a map," Aziza explained. "Look at the detail, Sultan. All the four corners of the world."

"And there's Agrabah," said the Sultan, pointing.

Aziza frowned. "But that's the ocean, Sultan."

"Of course it is," said the Sultan quickly. "I was just testing you." He caught Aziza's eye and jerked his turban toward the door. After several tries Aziza got the message.

"I must go to . . . to get a cup of tea," said Aziza, heading for the door. "But by the time I come back, I want you to have that problem figured out, Jasmine. Perhaps your father will help you."

Jasmine looked at her father. "If two camels are traveling in different directions, and one is carrying thirty pounds of lentils and the other has nine monkeys and a mouse on his back, which one will swim across the great river and reach Agrabah first?"

"Why does he have a mouse?" asked the Sultan.

"I don't know," Jasmine admitted.

"Then there can be no answer," the Sultan said, lying contentedly back on a couch, arms behind his head. Rajah hopped up beside him, laid his big orange head down on the Sultan's stomach, and promptly went to sleep.

"Rajah, you dear pussycat," the Sultan said, groaning under the big animal's weight. "When are you going to realize you're not a kitten anymore?" He shoved Rajah aside and cleared his

throat. "You know, Jasmine, you're growing up just as fast as Rajah! You'll be thinking about choosing a suitor before you know it." The Sultan sighed, his eyes misting over.

Jasmine made a face. "I'd rather think about swimming camels than suitors."

"Oh, I'm sure you'll change your mind about that, dearest. In the meantime you've got another birthday coming up soon."

But Jasmine was concentrating on the map. "Oh, Father, wouldn't it be wonderful to see everything on this map?" she said. "Not just Agrabah. There's a whole world outside these walls, just waiting for me to introduce myself. A whole world full of adventures!" She ran to the window, taking in the glorious view of the sprawling, bustling city and the desert beyond.

"Jasmine," the Sultan said gently. Rajah shifted positions and began to snore, drooling on the Sultan's shoulder. "Those sorts of adventures . . . well, they're not for you, dearest. You're a princess. Not a world explorer."

"But why, Father?" Jasmine turned and gazed at him beseechingly.

"Because, well . . ." The Sultan considered. "Princesses have always stayed within the palace."

"Why?"

"Because . . . because they're very important people. And they have to be protected."

"But that doesn't explain why I can never leave." Jasmine stared at him, hands on her hips. "I want to know why, Father."

The Sultan disentangled himself from the sleeping Rajah and stood, rubbing his temples. "I'm going downstairs. Suddenly I feel the need for some poppy-seed cake."

He went into the hallway. He still didn't have a clue what to get Jasmine for her birthday. On top of that, she had him feeling flustered and confused. "Where does she get all her questions from?" he wondered aloud.

That afternoon the Sultan went into the royal kitchen to snitch the last piece of poppy-seed cake. "My, you have such a fine healthy appetite, Sultan," said Safiya.

"Why thank you, Safiya," said the Sultan, licking frosting from his fingers.

"Nassir the tailor said you were trying to think of a gift for Jasmine," she said. "Have you come up with something? I am already planning her birthday cake. It will be the most wonderful cake ever baked. Ten cubits high, a hundred different layers."

The Sultan's eyes glazed over at the thought of such a magnificent cake. But then he remembered that he still had a problem to solve. "No, Safiya, I haven't decided on the perfect gift to go with your splendid . . . amazing . . . Did you say fifty layers?"

"A hundred layers," Safiya corrected.

"A hundred layers! My, my. I'm sure I shall enjoy . . . er, that is to say, *Jasmine* will enjoy . . . Where is that girl, anyway?"

"Talking to the fish peddler," Safiya said, shaking her head. She led the Sultan down a long, narrow hall from the kitchen to an entranceway where merchants brought food and wares to the palace. Jasmine was perched atop a pile of wooden crates, watching as a fisherman unloaded crates of big silver fish.

"Father!" she called as the Sultan approached. "Khalid was just telling me a wonderful story about how he caught a twenty-foot fish and then the fish nearly had him for dinner!"

"Thirty-foot, Princess," said the fisherman. "Not that I'm bragging."

"And look, Father," Jasmine said, waving a dark green glob. "Khalid gave me seaweed!" She inhaled deeply and sighed. "Is this how the ocean smells?"

Khalid nodded. "Yes, Princess, it smells of salt and sun. There are fish in all the colors of the rainbow. And pearls in the mouths of oysters. And mighty leviathans in the depths."

"I'm going to keep this seaweed in my bedchamber," Jasmine told her father, closing her eyes and breathing in the scent again. "It's like having a piece of the sea."

Safiya leaned close to the Sultan. "No wonder you can't think of anything to get her. She's got a piece of seaweed and I've never seen her so happy."

The Sultan frowned, then smiled. "I may know just what to get Jasmine after all," he whispered back.

* * *

On the morning of her birthday Jasmine was awakened suddenly by the trumpet of an elephant coming from the throne room just below her bedchamber. But that was crazy, of course. The only elephant in the throne room was the golden one decorating her father's throne. She must have been dreaming. She was a little tired—she and Rajah had stayed up late watching the stars, and she'd wished for the best birthday ever, for something wonderful and surprising and very out of the ordinary.

Still, that was unlikely, she thought as she dressed. Her father meant well, but he didn't always know what a young girl wanted. Last year he'd gotten her topaz-studded slippers—very uncomfortable, but of course she had pretended to love them.

One thing was certain—the Sultan had definitely been up to

something for the last few weeks. He'd been whispering and bustling about and just generally grinning a lot. And there was no telling what *that* meant.

"Jasmine dear, are you awake?" her father called. Jasmine opened the door. "Happy birthday!" the Sultan cried, giving her a hug. "Do you feel any older?"

"Not really," Jasmine admitted.

"Well, I do," said the Sultan. "You're growing up much too fast." He took her hand and led her down the long hall.

Rajah raced ahead, tail twitching, nose on alert. Jasmine hesitated. Rajah had very good instincts, and right now he looked concerned about something.

"What is that strange smell?" Jasmine asked.

"That?" the Sultan asked. "I believe that may be the scent of camels. But I mustn't give away the surprise!" He paused near the stairs. "Are you ready?"

"Of course," she said, a little nervously. "But where is it?"

"Everywhere," the Sultan said, grinning from ear to ear.

Jasmine took a step down the stairs. Rajah crept stealthily by her side. All was quiet below. She took two more steps. "Father?" she asked, turning.

"Since I couldn't bring you to the world," said the Sultan, "I brought the world to you!"

Suddenly, in a burst of color and noise, while Jasmine watched in absolute amazement, the palace came alive. Out from behind every nook and cranny appeared more people, more different, wonderful, strange, exotic people, than Jasmine's textbooks had ever allowed her even to imagine. They streamed into the main hall from every direction, laughing and singing in a torrent of unfamiliar tongues.

Chinese acrobats capered overhead on a stretched wire. African tribal dancers shook tall shields in time to frantic drums. Fur-clothed Norsemen carried on a mock sword fight. Six Persian jugglers sent knives slicing through the air. People of every description, white and red and yellow and black and brown, filled the palace to the roof with chaotic revelry.

Jasmine turned to the Sultan in mystified wonder, but before she could say anything she was sucked into the teeming throngs. She was carried forward into the throne room, which held a long row of booths where strange people cooked unfamiliar yet fragrant delicacies. Jasmine saw pies and pancakes, round cheeses and tiny little flowers of spun sugar, and, strangest of all, long edible strings called pasta. Everywhere she looked she saw jars of food, baskets of food, steaming pots of food.

"The food booths are my favorite part," the Sultan confided when he caught up with her.

Jasmine smiled at him, still unable to speak. She felt as if she'd been dropped into a marvelous, crazy dream. She left her father drooling over a display of pastries while she and Rajah made their way to the courtyard outside. On the way someone grabbed her arm and swung her around a maypole. Nearby, a band was playing on strange-looking instruments.

In the courtyard she found a host of wonderful animals she'd seen only in her books—a rhinoceros, a pair of hyenas, even a great fat hippopotamus. Rajah slunk up to an orangutan. They touched noses, and Rajah ran for cover. Iago, meanwhile, had been cornered by a hungry-looking lion. "Nice kitty-kitty-kitty!" he repeated over and over.

In the gardens Jasmine was stunned to find a huge stone monument that had been erected overnight. "It's—it's an Egyptian pyramid!" she cried in amazement. In the very center of the garden Jasmine discovered a miniature version of the Agrabah marketplace, just as it looked from her window. Sword swallowers

vied with trinket sellers for her attention. "Take a rest!" cried the man who slept on a bed of nails. A fortune-teller stared deep into a glass ball. Children played a noisy game of tag, dodging in and out among the booths. A camel salesman chatted with an old woman who was hanging her wash on a line.

At the center of the marketplace Jasmine found the Sultan again. The front of his tunic was stained with raspberries, and he was licking chocolate from his fingers. "Father!" she exclaimed. "This is amazing!"

"Did you see the rhinoceros?" he asked, his eyes as wide as hers. "And the pandas . . . and the . . . oh my, it is quite splendid, isn't it?"

Jasmine hugged him. "Quite splendid. What a wonderful surprise. It must have been so much work!"

"Dear me, yes. Of course, all my advisers helped. I supervised, which is what I do best. Why, when I woke up this morning there was a hippo in my bath, can you imagine? And Jafar had to share his room with a python. Actually, they got along very well."

Jasmine sank down onto the edge of the fountain to rest. Suddenly she gasped. Colorful, glimmering tropical fish were swimming in lazy circles like dozens of tiny rainbows. She leaned over and breathed in deeply, then smiled. "It's filled with . . . "

"Seawater," the Sultan finished with a nod. "It took twenty camels to transport it."

Jasmine reached down into the fountain, then tasted her fingertips. Salt! Her father had even brought the ocean to her.

"You're the very best father in the world," Jasmine said, her eyes filling with tears of joy as she hugged him again. "And this is the best present in the world. It *is* the world!"

The Sultan smiled contentedly. All his hard work had paid off.

Jasmine gazed at the wondrous variety of activities, people, animals, and things around her. She didn't tell her father, but his gift had made her more determined than ever to find a way to travel outside the palace one day. And when she did, she knew she'd never get tired of seeing all the world had to offer.

Prince for a Day

I t was a fine, peaceful morning, so hot that even the flies were dozing in the shade. Aladdin and Abu made their way through the marketplace at a jaunty pace, waving to friends and hiding from patrolling guards.

Suddenly there was a frightened cry. "Runaway camel!" someone screamed. "Look out!"

Aladdin turned just in time to see a huge camel galloping through the marketplace, a panicked expression on its face, sending people scurrying to get out of its way. On its back a little boy hung on for dear life, his terrified screams almost lost in the thunder of hooves.

"Stop him!" cried a well-dressed man riding in a luxurious palanquin. "That's my child!"

The camel knocked over a wagon, spilling a river of pomegranates. The shoemaker's stand tumbled, burying the poor man beneath a mountain of shoes. A family of mangy street dogs dove for cover under a pile of carpets.

"Help me!" the little boy cried. "He won't stop!"

Aladdin looked at Abu. "Feeling heroic?" he asked.

With Abu clinging to his shoulder, Aladdin raced after the camel. "Look out, Aladdin!" cried Halima, the old woman who sometimes gave Aladdin leftovers from her kitchen. "He'll trample you!"

Aladdin gained speed, took a detour, and clambered up a huge pyramid of melons. From atop the pile he could see the camel coming. He could also see that the little boy was losing his grip. At any moment he could fall and be crushed beneath the camel's hooves.

With Abu still holding on tight, Aladdin leaped off the pile as the camel galloped by. The melons went rolling in all directions. Aladdin grabbed the camel's neck and hung on upside down as the frightened animal picked up speed.

Dangling off the neck of the camel was a little like riding a racehorse upside down. It took all of Aladdin's strength to climb aboard. He steadied the little boy, then grabbed hold of the reins and tugged at them. But the camel didn't even seem to feel it.

"Now it's your turn, Abu," Aladdin shouted.

Abu clambered up the camel's long neck to its head. He covered the camel's eyes with his paws. Immediately the panicked animal slowed to a stop.

"Nice work, Abu," Aladdin cried.

"Imran!" The man from the palanquin came running toward them. He gathered the boy into his arms, then turned to Aladdin. "You are a most brave and quick-thinking young man," he said gratefully.

"Aw, it was nothing," Aladdin said. Abu looked up and scowled at Aladdin. "Oh yeah," Aladdin added. "Abu here deserves some of the credit, too."

Abu removed his fez and gave a sweeping bow.

"I am Sheik Jamar of Algipur," said the man. He beckoned to

a servant and whispered something.

Sheik Jamar of Algipur? Aladdin stared at his beautiful silk robes and fine jewels. Was it possible? He was one of the wealthiest men in the land.

A moment later the sheik's servant returned with a large leather pouch. "You must take this," the sheik said, handing the pouch to Aladdin, "as a token of my gratitude."

"Well, if you absolutely insist," Aladdin said, eyeing the pouch eagerly. He hoped there was money or something to eat inside.

The sheik thanked them once more, then led his son away. Aladdin and Abu settled down in a quiet spot in the shade near Halima's kitchen door. Aladdin opened the pouch and looked inside.

"So?" asked Halima, walking over. "Was that wild stunt worth it, you crazy boy?"

"Crazy *rich* boy," Aladdin corrected, his eyes bright. He reached into the pouch and pulled out a handful of gold coins. "Abu," he breathed, "this is enough to let us eat forever!"

Abu peered deep into the pouch. When he pulled out his head he was grinning from ear to ear.

"Well, well," said Halima, shaking her head. "So Aladdin the urchin is rich? What will you do with all this wealth?"

Aladdin considered. "I think our first stop should be Nassir the tailor's. A rich young man must look like he's rich!" He gave Halima a jaunty wave, then hurried off with Abu. As they headed for Nassir's, Aladdin thought of all the wonderful things he could buy now. If he was careful, he might not need to steal or beg again for a long time—maybe forever!

Nassir's shop was piled high with silks of every color. When the tailor saw Aladdin and Abu walk in the door, he threw up his hands. "Shoo! Scat!" he growled. "I've no work for you, street rat! Get away before you scare off the real customers.

You know—the ones with *money*?"

Aladdin grinned. He was used to being chased off by the merchants of the bazaar. But today was different. Today he was officially no longer a street rat. He opened the pouch and gave it a jingle. "Money, you say?"

"Why, this is real gold!" Nassir cried as he peered inside. His dark eyes narrowed. "What did you do to get this, rob a nobleman?"

"That's not a very nice way to talk to a rich young customer who wants to buy a whole new wardrobe," Aladdin said.

"You are absolutely right," Nassir said. "And nothing is too fine for my excellent friend Aladdin."

Nassir paraded all his finest wares, and Aladdin tried on everything. Meanwhile, Abu tried on some children's clothing. It was all far too large, but Nassir cinched a belt around the monkey's waist and assured him that he looked positively elegant.

Finally Aladdin and Abu were decked out in stylish new finery, right down to a new tasseled fez for Abu. Aladdin stood before a mirror with Abu on his shoulder, admiring their new look.

Nassir held up a tight bundle. "Your old clothes, sir."

Aladdin waved his hand. "Away with them. Toss them into the trash where they belong." He spied a veil, spun as sheer and iridescent as a spider's dew-covered web. "I'll take that, too," he said. Abu grabbed the veil and wound it around his neck. "Very dashing, Abu," said Aladdin. "But that's a gift for Halima."

Just then a rotund gentleman with a pointed beard and a brisk gait entered. Aladdin recognized him as Rahim, one of the richest merchants in Agrabah. Aladdin had once been chased from Rahim's shop when Abu had tried to swipe a bunch of bananas with his tail. Aladdin started to duck away, but Rahim just gazed at him curiously, taking in Aladdin's expensive clothes with a look of admiration.

"Nassir, my worthy friend," said Rahim, "aren't you going to introduce me to this fine young gentleman?"

"Allow me to introduce myself," said Aladdin, relieved that Rahim didn't seem to recognize him. "I am Aladdin, and this is my dear friend Abu."

Rahim nodded politely. "And where do you hail from?"

"From . . ." Aladdin hesitated. "From a higher elevation north of town." It was true, in a way. The abandoned rooftop where he lived was in the northern section of the marketplace.

"I see you share my taste in finery," Rahim said, pointing to Aladdin's new turban. "You must be an apprentice to a businessman, I'm guessing? Perhaps a trader? A merchant, like myself?"

"In a way," Aladdin said. "I . . . uh, I'm in the food relocation business." Also technically true, although mostly he relocated food from merchants' stalls into his own stomach.

"Well, we must get together. There's no telling what we might come up with. Some commerce, perhaps. You are clearly a smart, capable young man. Would you do me the honor of dining at my home tonight?"

"I—me?"

Abu jumped onto Aladdin's shoulder and smiled winningly.

"You and your . . . friend. He doesn't bite, does he?" Rahim patted Abu's head. "Nice monkey." Abu patted Rahim's head back. Rahim recoiled. "I live on the corner near Abdullah the fortune-teller's tent. The big house. You can't miss it."

"We'll be there," said Aladdin with a cocky smile.

Aladdin and Abu swaggered happily through the marketplace until they found Halima hanging out her wash. "You must be looking for Fawad the diamond merchant," she said as they approached. She blinked. Then she rubbed her eyes and looked again. "Aladdin! Why, you devil! I'd have thought you were the Sultan himself."

"And you will now look like a princess," Aladdin said. He reached out and draped the veil he'd bought around Halima's neck.

"Oh, Aladdin, you silly boy. You shouldn't have." She fingered the beautiful veil. "Still, I'm glad you did. Thank you." Halima hesitated. "But if you keep spending like this, you'll be broke by the end of the day."

"I'll be careful," Aladdin said.

"You should save the rest of your money for the essentials," Halima warned.

"Essentials," Aladdin promised.

Abu and Aladdin headed back into the marketplace. "The first essential is, I'm essentially very hungry. How about you, Abu?"

Abu rubbed his stomach, nodding hopefully.

Minutes later Aladdin and Abu were whisked off to the finest outdoor table at Amir's Famous Shish-K-Bab. Waiters gathered around the pair as if they were royalty. "Can you believe this?" Aladdin said as Abu scanned the menu. Abu couldn't read, but

he liked the pictures. "Just yesterday we were eating Shish-K-Leftovers."

Just then Aladdin felt a cold, wet nose against his hand. He looked up from his menu to see a family of mangy dogs—the very ones he'd seen scurry from the camel earlier—slinking under his table.

"Miserable curs," said the waiter, rushing up. "I'm most sorry, sir. The little beggars drive us crazy."

Little beggars. How many times had Aladdin heard that same phrase directed at him and Abu?

"That's all right, waiter," Aladdin said in his most authoritative voice. "These dogs are my guests."

"Your . . . guests?"

"That's right. They'll be dining with me today." Aladdin pulled back chairs, and the dogs hopped up. One of the puppies squeezed in beside Abu.

"We'll have your Amir's Specialty-Bab, one for each of us," said Aladdin with a smile. "And don't forget the doggy bags."

An hour later everyone had a round stomach and a smile on his face. It was a wonderful feeling, Aladdin thought, seeing the dogs and Abu so well fed and content. And it wasn't half bad feeling so content himself.

All that afternoon Aladdin and Abu wandered the streets. Whenever he ran into one of his friends, Aladdin would tell his story, and inevitably he'd end up giving away some of his money. How could he resist? Naki needed a new pair of crutches. Jamila's sandals were so full of holes that her feet were blistered. Hafez needed a new blanket for the cold desert nights. The roof of Yahiya's little hut had blown away in a sandstorm.

As the late-afternoon shadows lengthened, Aladdin sat at the edge of the marketplace with Abu. Spending money was hard work, and they were both looking forward to dinner at Rahim's house.

"Well, how do you like being rich, Abu?" Aladdin asked. "It's funny. People treat me differently. They bow and smile and make way for me. But I don't feel any different. Maybe it takes a while to get used to."

He raised the pouch. Somehow *it* felt different. Strangely light. He opened the pouch and reached inside. But something was missing. His money! The pouch was empty!

Aladdin turned the pouch over and over, looking for a hole. "It must have fallen out," he said. "I couldn't have spent it all—"

Abu crossed his arms, looking at Aladdin reproachfully.

"—could I?" Aladdin asked. He remembered Halima's warning and groaned. How could he have been so foolish? "I'm sorry, Abu," he said. "I guess it's back to scrounging for us tomorrow. But at least we'll get one more good meal out of it at Rahim's tonight. Come on, let's go."

Abu nodded and jumped to his feet, patting his stomach hungrily.

"Everything will still work out fine, Abu," Aladdin said confidently as they set off for Rahim's house. "After all, Rahim said we could do business together. Didn't he say I was a smart, capable young man? Surely he'll have a job for a smart, capable guy like me."

From the darkness of an alley Aladdin heard a tiny voice call his name. Two little street waifs were huddled in the far corner, shivering in the cold that was seeping into the marketplace with the deepening shadows. "Ahmad? Efra?" Aladdin called. "Is that you?"

The children waved at him, their teeth chattering. Just then Aladdin had a wonderful idea. "Abu, follow me." He ran back down the alley to the trash can behind Nassir's and began to dig through the smelly trash. Abu held his nose. The alley held all-too-familiar odors.

"Aha!" Aladdin cried at last. He displayed a small bundle. "Our old rags!"

As he realized what Aladdin had in mind, Abu shook his head and crossed his arms over his chest. No way was he giving up his new tasseled fez. "Come on, Abu," Aladdin chided, quickly changing into his old clothes. "Efra would love that vest of yours. It's too big for you, anyway."

A few minutes later Efra and Ahmad were running up and down the alley dressed in their new finery. Aladdin's clothes were a little too big for Ahmad, Abu's a little too small for Efra, but they didn't mind. They were warm and clean.

Aladdin smiled with satisfaction. His old clothes might not be very fancy, but they were still comfortable. And now that he was poor again, who cared what he wore?

Just a few minutes ahead of schedule Aladdin and Abu climbed the stairs to Rahim's fine house. Bright lights glimmered behind the windows. Aladdin could only imagine what a meal at such a house must taste like. It would probably be almost like dining at the palace.

"Be on your best behavior, Abu," Aladdin warned.

The big door swung open. Behind a servant stood Rahim. "We don't feed beggars," the servant said.

"Yes, be off," said Rahim. "Get away from my door."

"But you invited us," said Aladdin.

"Invited? Nonsense!" Rahim cried. "Why would I invite a street rat into my home?"

"You said I was smart and . . . and capable."

"Don't be absurd. I've never met you before in my life."

The door slammed shut. "I guess our dinner plans just got canceled, Abu," said Aladdin angrily. He shook his fist at the door. "That son of a jackal! I won't always be a street rat," he shouted. "Someday you'll be sorry, Rahim."

For a long time Aladdin and Abu wandered through the empty marketplace in the velvet blue twilight. How could he have made such a mess of things? Aladdin wondered. He could have eaten forever on all that money. Instead he'd spent most of it on other people. He shook his head, angry with himself. He knew he'd given Yahiya twice what he needed to repair his roof. And Naki could buy four new crutches with the amount he'd given her. He should have been more careful. It had just been so wonderful to do something nice for his friends.

Finally, as the stars began to appear in the sky, Aladdin and Abu headed for home. They climbed slowly up the long staircase that led to their rooftop home, feeling weary and hungry and more than a little foolish.

Halfway up, Aladdin paused. He was sure he'd heard something. A noise? It wasn't likely anyone would try to rob his humble abode. But still, it paid to be careful.

Stealthily Aladdin crept up the stairs, Abu on his shoulder. When he reached the top, he was amazed at what he saw. Candles glowed on a long board that had been set on two rocks as a makeshift table. Halima's beautiful new veil covered it like a tablecloth. Naki was there, and Jamila and Hafez and Yahiya—all the people Aladdin had given money to that day. Even the dogs who'd dined with Aladdin and Abu were there, playing with Efra and Ahmad.

"What's going on?" Aladdin asked.

"We're having a party in your honor," said Halima. "You're our hero, Aladdin." Abu cleared his throat. "And you, too, Abu," Halima added, laughing.

"Everyone took a bit of the money you gave us and bought something," Jamila explained. "It's not much—nothing as fancy as you would have had at Rahim's—but there are dates and melons and day-old bread, and Yahiya even found some goat cheese."

"How did you know I wasn't eating at Rahim's?" Aladdin asked.

"Ahmad saw what happened," Halima said. "He told me, I told Hafez . . . word travels swiftly in the marketplace, Aladdin."

"But you all should have saved the extra money for essentials," Aladdin said. "That's what you told me to do."

"Instead you gave it to people who needed it even more than you did," Halima said, smiling.

Aladdin shrugged. "I guess that was the most essential thing I could think of."

"Well, saying thank you is essential, too," Halima replied.

Everyone sat down to enjoy the feast. When all had eaten their fill, Aladdin played his flute while Abu danced on the

table. There was laughter and singing and much merriment, and the party went on until dawn.

From time to time Aladdin would glance out and see the palace glowing in the moonlight. When he'd been rich, those gleaming towers had seemed just a little bit closer somehow; now they looked as distant as ever.

But at this moment, surrounded by his friends, he felt like a prince nonetheless.

That Magical Feeling

Jasmine shinnied her way up the slender trunk of the tallest date palm in the palace gardens. Although her father disapproved of her climbing like this—he said it was undignified—Jasmine loved the commanding view it gave her of Agrabah and the world beyond.

She scanned the horizon nervously. "Today's the day, Rajah," she said to the big tiger who was waiting patiently on the ground below. "My first suitor. Everyone says he's perfectly nice. Very handsome. I hope they're right." She sighed. "But what if they're wrong?"

Rajah raised his head and growled his most ferocious growl. He had no idea what a suitor was, but no matter. He'd protect Jasmine regardless of the threat.

"I know the law says it's time for me to start thinking about getting married, but sometimes laws are wrong. . . ."

A whirlwind of sand, like a small tornado, appeared on the horizon. Camels!

"Oh, Rajah, I'll bet that's Prince Omar!" Jasmine gulped. "What if he doesn't like me? What if I can't think of a thing to

say to him? What if he takes one look at me and says I look like a gargoyle? What if—"

"Jasmine! Confound it, girl! What are you doing up in that tree?"

Jasmine looked down to see her father, looking red-faced and flustered. "I think I see Prince Omar, Father."

"Please, hurry down now, dearest," the Sultan pleaded. "You're not even dressed yet! What will he think if he sees you up there? Prince Omar is from a very prominent family. His father Hassan and I are old and dear friends, so I want you to be on your best behavior. Positively no tree climbing."

"I promise, Father," Jasmine said, climbing down. "No trees until he leaves."

"Omar is a very fine young man, trust me. In fact, he's the most eligible bachelor in Aquitar. And what's more, Jafar says it would make for a very nice alliance if you and Prince Omar married." The Sultan shooed Jasmine toward the palace. "Come, come. You mustn't delay any longer."

In her bedchamber Jasmine donned her new robes of the finest shimmering silk. She combed her hair carefully and checked her reflection in a looking glass. Then she combed her hair again. Finally she looked at Rajah with a resigned sigh.

"Well, I've done my best not to look like a gargoyle, Rajah." She threw back her shoulders. "Let's go meet my suitor."

Jasmine headed downstairs, feeling a dizzying mixture of curiosity, dread, and excitement. Suppose she really did end up falling head over heels for this perfect stranger? It could happen, after all. It had happened that way for her mother and father.

As Jasmine reached the hall leading to the reception room the Sultan came hurrying out, looking most agitated. "There you are, dearest! I was beginning to think you'd run off."

"Why would I do that?" Jasmine asked, peering over his shoulder.

"Why—no reason!" the Sultan said quickly. "Come, come. Meet Omar." He paused. "But promise me one thing. You'll give him a chance."

"Of course I will," Jasmine promised.

The Sultan took Jasmine by the hand and led her into the reception room. She held her breath. If her mother had fallen in love this way, maybe she would, too. . . .

"Prince Omar of Aquitar—Princess Jasmine of Agrabah," the Sultan said.

Jasmine blinked in disbelief.

Omar was sprawled out on a couch. His turban was on sideways. His hair stuck out at odd angles like an overused broom. His robe was stained and wrinkled.

"Prince Omar?" Jasmine said uncertainly.

"In the flesh. Is it okay if I call you Jaz?"

"I—um, I suppose so." Jasmine took a deep breath. This, *this* was the most eligible bachelor in Aquitar? She sent her father a questioning glance.

"Omar's changed quite a bit since the last time I saw him," said the Sultan a bit sheepishly.

"How's that, Sul? You mind if I call you Sul?"

"Well," said the Sultan. "You're taller, for one thing."

"Plus I got a tattoo," Omar volunteered. "Wanna see?"

"Oh my, no," said the Sultan quickly. He cleared his throat. "Well, I suppose I should leave you two to get acquainted—"

"Father!" Jasmine said, teeth clenched.

"I'll just be in the next room if you need me," the Sultan said reassuringly. He bent closer to whisper in Jasmine's ear. "Remember, give him a chance. You know what they say—don't judge a book by its cover."

"So, Jaz," Omar said as the Sultan departed. "You're scrawnier than I figured." He lowered his voice. "Especially with that old man of yours. Tell me the truth. Is that really his stomach, or does he store a pillow in there?"

"Now wait just a minute!" Jasmine cried, but she was interrupted by the entrance of a servant carrying a tea tray.

Omar grabbed a cup of tea and took a loud slurp. Tea dribbled down his chin, leaving a brown trail on his robes. He wiped his mouth on his sleeve.

"Hey," he said as the servant left. "About that crack about the old man—no offense."

Jasmine sipped her tea without answering. Perhaps Omar was just nervous. "Is your tea satisfactory?" she asked coolly.

"This tea isn't bad, although I like the way we serve it in Aquitar better."

"And how is that?"

"We put a big red worm in the bottom of the teacup. The first person to eat the worm gets to make a wish."

Jasmine gasped. "You eat the worm?"

"A little lemon, some sugar, it really hits the spot. You'll get used to it. It's the traditional drink of Aquitar."

Just then Rajah wandered in, eyeing the prince skeptically. "Rajah!" Jasmine said happily. "Prince Omar, meet—"

"Yeoww!" The prince leaped onto a table and lurched for a chandelier.

"Really, Rajah's perfectly harmless," Jasmine assured him. "He's my pet."

"Get that mangy beast out of here!" Omar cried, swinging to and fro on the chandelier.

Rajah positioned himself beneath the prince, his head slowly moving back and forth while he watched Omar sway like a pendulum.

"Rajah's my best friend in the world," Jasmine said firmly,

arms crossed. "You might as well get used to him."

"He wants to eat me, I'm telling you," Omar screeched.

"Nonsense. Rajah wouldn't do that." Jasmine smiled sweetly. "Not unless I told him to. Now come down from there, Omar. You look ridiculous."

"No way." Omar was shaking so hard the glass chandelier tinkled like bells. Jasmine sighed. As unlikable as he was, it was hard not to feel just a little bit sorry for him.

"Rajah," she said. "Come sit here next to me."

Rajah yawned and sat calmly beside Jasmine. "It's safe now, Omar," Jasmine called.

Omar considered, then let go of the chandelier and landed—*splat*—on top of the table. It splintered into a million pieces, and Omar went sprawling onto the floor.

"Cheap furniture," he commented as he stood, brushing himself off. He sat down cautiously on a nearby chair, his eyes locked on Rajah's. "You know, you'll have to get rid of that—that mouth with fur—if we get married," he said, pulling a splinter out of his turban.

"Who said anything about getting married?" Jasmine cried.

"It's what our fathers want, face it," said the prince. Jasmine thought she heard something wistful in his voice, but in an instant it vanished. "Anyway," Omar continued, "my point is, I have a family of pet rats who sleep with me at night. Put a cat and a rat in the same room and, well, I'm sure you see the problem."

"First of all, where I go, Rajah goes," Jasmine said. "And secondly, who in his right mind has rats for pets?"

"These are not just any rats. As a matter of fact, they're so smart I taught them to fetch my slippers in the morning." He gulped down the rest of his tea. "Of course, it takes a couple of hours, but it's most entertaining."

Jasmine cleared her throat. She glanced over her shoulder, wondering if she could escape without anyone noticing. But no. She'd promised her father she'd be on her best behavior. "So," she said, trying her best to sound interested, "what else do you do for entertainment in Aquitar?"

"Not much. I pretty much never leave the palace, what with the flooding."

"Flooding?"

"We live in a valley on the banks of a river. Floods pretty much every other week. By the time we get the mud bailed out, we flood again."

"Why don't you move the palace?"

"Oh, you get used to it. When the water gets too deep you just take a raft from room to room." He eyed her speculatively. "So, Jaz, enough about me. Tell me a little about yourself."

Jasmine hesitated and looked down at her hands. "Well, I . . . I like to talk to all the people who come to the palace because I'm very interested in the outside world. Someday I'm going to—"

A deafening, guttural snore interrupted her words. Jasmine looked over to see that Prince Omar was fast asleep.

"I cannot believe how rude he is!" Jasmine cried, leaping to her feet. "Rajah, you stay here and make sure he doesn't steal anything. I'm going to talk to Father."

Jasmine stormed down the hall to the throne room, where the Sultan was talking with Aziza and Jafar.

"Enjoying your little date, Princess?" Jafar asked.

"No, I am *not* enjoying it!" Jasmine cried. "Father, Prince Omar is the most disgusting, rude, ill-mannered, self-centered, offensive, ill-bred, vulgar—" She paused for air.

"Might I suggest boorish?" Aziza added.

"And not only that, he's just plain weird!"

"Now, now, Jasmine," said the Sultan, patting her on the arm, "I know the young man's a bit, well, unkempt, but perhaps that's the style in Aquitar. Or maybe he's going through a phase. Youngsters can be so rebellious these days."

"They eat worms in Aquitar, Father! And they ride around the palace on rafts!" She threw up her hands. "And did you see the way he looks?"

"You know, Jasmine," said the Sultan, "I have to admit that this isn't the same Omar I met the last time I visited Aquitar. He was a most well mannered boy then. Still, I hate to judge him too hastily, since his father and I are such good friends—"

"Father. He sleeps with rats."

The Sultan sighed. "Well then, I suppose we'll just have to send him on his way. Dear me, what will I ever tell Hassan?"

"Tell him his son needs some manners. And a bath wouldn't hurt, either," Jasmine said. "I'll go tell Omar good-bye. It'll be the most fun I've had today."

At least this nightmare is almost over, Jasmine told herself as she marched back to the reception room. To think that Omar had had the nerve to call her scrawny! And to insult the Sultan! Why, it was almost as if he had been *trying* to annoy her.

Suddenly Jasmine stopped short and gasped. The reception room looked as if a mighty windstorm had swept through it. Chairs and tables were overturned, vases in splinters, pictures askew. A large pillow sat on the floor, a hole in its center just about the size of Rajah's mouth. A shredded piece of Omar's robe lay nearby.

There was only one answer. Rajah had eaten Omar.

"Rajah!" Jasmine cried, dashing across the room to the door leading to the gardens. How was she ever going to explain this to her father?

"Omar!" she screamed, zigzagging through the bushes.

She heard a shout. Omar's voice! At least he was still alive. Jasmine ran in the direction of the shout, dreading what she would see when she got there.

She rounded a hedge and gasped. Rajah and Omar were splashing in a fountain, playing tug-of-war with a pillow, obviously having a marvelous time.

"Rajah?" Jasmine cried in stunned disbelief. "What are you doing playing with Omar?" This made no sense at all. Rajah had always been an excellent judge of character.

Omar dropped the pillow and leaped to the ground. His grin evaporated. "He . . . this monster tried to attack me! I've been

68

fending him off. I tell you, he's vicious!"

Rajah looked confused. Then his golden eyes lit up. He stood up on his hind legs, dropped his big paws on Omar's shoulders, and planted a long lick on the prince's nose.

"Stop!" Omar protested. "Stop, you wild—" But Rajah kept licking, and before long Omar dissolved into a gale of laughter. "Stop him!" he begged Jasmine, rolling on the ground. "He's tickling me! Stop him before I laugh to death."

"That's enough, Rajah," Jasmine said, and the big tiger moved away reluctantly. "What exactly is going on here, Omar? One minute you're terrified of Rajah, and as soon as I leave the room you two are the best of friends. How do you explain that?"

"Chemistry?" Omar offered. He sat up and tried to straighten his turban.

Jasmine perched on the side of the fountain. "Omar, Rajah is very discriminating. If he likes you, there must be a reason. Not that I can begin to imagine what it is."

Omar groaned. "Asha told me this would never work." He paused to wring some water from his robes. "She said you would see through to my inner charm."

"Actually," Jasmine said, smiling, "she overestimated my abilities. Who is Asha, anyway?"

"My . . ." Omar looked away. His eyes misted over.

"Omar? You can tell me."

"Asha is my one true love in all the world," Omar said, his voice choked with emotion. "The sweetest girl in Aquitar! She is more lovely than a desert blossom, more precious than diamonds. . . ." He sighed. "We are in love, Jasmine. But my father wants me to marry you because it would make a good alliance. I told him no, I cannot marry for reasons like that. I have to marry for love. But he wouldn't listen."

70

"So you came here, hoping to make me dislike you so there wouldn't be a chance of our marrying?" Jasmine said. "How underhanded! How devious."

"You have every right to be angry. I am ashamed."

"No, no, I'm impressed," Jasmine said, laughing. "It was a brilliant plan, Omar." She paused. "Although you went a little too far with that scrawny remark."

"The truth," said Omar, blushing slightly, "is that your beauty is blinding, Jasmine. But in my heart there is room only for Asha."

Jasmine sighed. "This is so romantic! I've got to help you somehow, Omar. If I refuse you, will you be free to marry Asha?"

"That is what my father promised."

"Well, then consider yourself refused."

Omar grinned from ear to ear. "Jasmine, you are a very special girl." He grasped her hands thankfully. "Promise me you won't allow yourself to be forced into marrying. True love is worth waiting for."

"Is it very wonderful?" Jasmine asked. "Being in love?"

Omar nodded and smiled. "Have you ever had a dream where you were flying?"

"Once," Jasmine said, closing her eyes at the memory. "I was high over Agrabah, floating on the breeze. It was the most incredible, dizzy, magical feeling!"

"That," said Omar, "is exactly what being in love is like."

Jasmine stroked Rajah's head. "I wonder if anyone will ever love me the way you love Asha."

Omar stood and reached down to help her to her feet. "Well, I'm no fortune-teller," he said, "but I think there will be true love in your future, Jasmine. You just have to wait for the right person."

"Come on," Jasmine said with a smile. "We'd better go tell Father you're not my right person."

The next morning Jasmine and the Sultan stood on a balcony, watching Omar and his entourage depart.

Omar climbed on his camel and waved. "See ya, Jaz," he said with a wink.

The Sultan shook his head sadly. "He used to be such a nice boy."

"Oh, he wasn't all bad," Jasmine said with a philosophical shrug. "At least now I know what I *don't* want in a suitor." She gazed out at Agrabah and sighed. Was there really true love in her future, as Omar had foretold?

"Poor Omar," said the Sultan. "I predict that boy will never marry. Who would have him?"

"I don't know, Father. I think there's a perfect match for everyone out there in the world somewhere." Jasmine leaned out over the railing as far as she dared. For a moment she felt a dizzy, magical, weightless feeling, a feeling like flying . . . or maybe even like being in love.

"All you have to do," she whispered, "is find him."

Fame and Fortune

I've got you this time, you little thieves!"

His sword poised, Rasoul, the head of the Sultan's guard, glared down at Aladdin and Abu. Aladdin was holding a skewer of sizzling hot lamb he'd sneaked off a vendor's grill.

"What do you have to say for yourself, street rat?" Rasoul boomed.

"Uh . . . catch?" Aladdin tossed the hot skewer to Rasoul, who caught it automatically.

"Yeoww!" he bellowed.

Aladdin and Abu made a mad dash through the crowded marketplace with Rasoul hot on their trail. Up ahead, Aladdin noticed Abdullah the fortune-teller sitting cross-legged in his tent, gazing into his crystal ball.

"Hey, Abdullah," Aladdin said, sliding to a breathless halt. "Mind if we stop and visit?"

"Not at all. I had a feeling you were coming," said Abdullah, a little wisp of a man with a long gray beard whose talents included fortune-telling, sword swallowing, and fire breathing.

Aladdin spotted two very large brass vases. "Swan dive!" he called to Abu. They each dove into a vase headfirst.

"Where are the little devils?" Rasoul demanded as he ran to Abdullah. "The monkey and the boy, have you seen them?"

"No monkeys, no boys."

The guard looked around with narrowed eyes. Aladdin and Abu held their breath. Finally Rasoul shrugged. "You'd better not be lying, old man," he threatened. "I'll be keeping my eye on you."

When the guard was gone, Abu and Aladdin climbed out of the vases. "Thanks, Abdullah," Aladdin said.

Abdullah waved his hand. "Don't thank me. I had a feeling it would turn out that way. It was fate."

Aladdin winked at Abu. "Hey, Abdullah, since you're so good at seeing the future, maybe you could predict where Abu and I are going to find lunch."

Abdullah raised one eyebrow. "Are you certain that you really want to know your future, Aladdin?" he asked. "What if your future is dark?"

"It can't be much darker than it is now," Aladdin said with a laugh.

"Then I will tell you what your future holds," Abdullah said. He gazed intently into his crystal ball. "I see much better things for you ahead. You will have powerful friends who . . . no, this can't be right. I'm seeing someone large and blue. Never mind that. Sometimes I get a little distortion in the signal." Suddenly he blinked and looked up in surprise. "Astounding," he said.

"Astounding? What kind of astounding?" Aladdin asked. "Astoundingly *good* or astoundingly *bad*?"

"I see a future where you will be astoundingly rich and powerful. You will have astounding adventures. And best of all, you will be in love with an astounding girl." Abdullah shook his head. "I have never seen such a completely astounding future in my crystal ball."

"Wow," Aladdin said, his eyes gleaming. "Rich and powerful, huh?"

"And in love," Abdullah reminded him.

"Uh-huh," Aladdin said with a wave. "That's nice, I guess. But I hope the rich and powerful part comes first." He leaned back and closed his eyes. He could already picture himself dressed in princely clothes, riding a spirited white horse—or better yet, an elephant. He could imagine dining with kings in splendid palaces and traveling the world in search of adventure.

"Uh-oh," Abdullah said, interrupting Aladdin's daydreams. "It looks as though your friend is returning. I had a feeling he might."

Aladdin looked where the fortune-teller was pointing and saw Rasoul coming toward them, an angry look on his face. Four more guards accompanied him, their swords drawn.

"Come on, Abu," Aladdin said. "Time to disappear." Aladdin grabbed Abu, and they dove under Abdullah's rug.

"Abdullah!" Rasoul thundered. "Up with you!"

"Me?" Abdullah asked.

"Him?" Aladdin whispered to Abu, peeking out from under the rug.

"But what have I done?" Abdullah asked. "I am but a poor fortune-teller—"

"You are but a rich thief!" Rasoul replied, grabbing the little man and reaching into the pocket of his robe. When he pulled out his hand, it held a large red ruby. "I just received a complaint about you."

Abdullah looked embarrassed. "The owner of that jewel called me a fake and a false magician. Naturally, I decided to make the ruby disappear from his pocket and appear in mine."

"You can tell that story to the Sultan when he judges you," Rasoul said.

As they dragged him away, Abdullah called out to Kareem the rug vendor. "Tell Aladdin, wherever he is, that he may have all my belongings until I am freed. But remind him to be careful. Seeing the future can be tricky!"

When the coast was clear, Aladdin and Abu crawled out from under the rug, Abdullah's words still ringing in their ears. Aladdin surveyed his inheritance. A carpet, a crystal ball, some magic tricks. A stick for fire breathing. A sword for swallowing. Balls for juggling. "I think we should stick to fortune-telling," he said to Abu. "It looks the least hazardous."

He was sorry for Abdullah's problems, but he knew he couldn't do anything to help. Sooner or later Abdullah would be back, but in the meantime this was Aladdin's lucky day. He could start earning his fortune as a fortune-teller.

Aladdin rummaged through an old trunk. He found an ancient-looking turban and a book. "*EZ Magic Tricks to Amaze and Amuse Your Friends,*" Aladdin read. Since the book was full of pictures, he gave it to Abu to examine. For his part, Aladdin settled cross-legged in front of the crystal ball. Was it possible Abdullah really could see the future in this simple glass sphere?

He squinted. The glass ball caught the bright noonday sun and reflected back its brilliant white light. Aladdin concentrated hard, staring deep into the ball even though the glare was hurting his eyes. He murmured the chant he'd heard Abdullah use. But he saw nothing.

"Oh well," he said to Abu at last. "When in doubt, improvise. How hard can it be? I'll just tell people what they want to hear, without promising them too much."

Abu shrugged, looking a little skeptical. Then he returned to his book.

"Fortunes! Get your red-hot fortunes!" Aladdin called out to the people hurrying past. "Two fortunes for the price of one!"

But no one stopped. After an hour of yelling, Aladdin was starting to get hoarse. He decided to improve his offer. "Satisfaction guaranteed or your money back!" he cried.

Abu looked at him doubtfully.

"What can it hurt?" Aladdin said. "As long as I'm careful what I say."

Suddenly Aladdin realized that a tall, solemn-looking, rather heavyset young man was staring at him with interest. Aladdin nudged Abu. "There he is!" he whispered. "Our first customer." He turned to the stranger with a broad smile. "Honored sir," Aladdin said. "Do you wish your fortune told?"

The young man blushed. "Well, er—I suppose it could be interesting," he said. His voice was low and serious. "I have been wondering quite a lot about my future lately."

"Then please, sit right down," Aladdin said. Abu rushed to lay out a cushion for the young man.

"My name is—" The young man paused. "But wait. If you truly have the power to see the future, you should know my name."

"Uh, of course," Aladdin said. "Let me see. Your name is . . . Mahmud?"

"No."

"Um, Hassan?"

"No."

"Kalif?"

To Aladdin's surprise the young man exclaimed, "Yes! My name is Kalif!" For just a second he gave Aladdin a small smile. Then his face regained its serious expression. "Your powers must truly be wonderful."

Aladdin sighed with relief at his luck. He could have gone on guessing for hours. "Well then, Kalif. Let me just gaze into my crystal ball, and we'll see what your future holds."

Aladdin rolled his eyes and waved his arms around a bit, just as he had seen Abdullah do. Then he gazed into the crystal sphere. At first he didn't see anything. Then he saw a face—a hairy face with big eyes.

It was Abu, staring into the other side of the ball.

"Abu! I'm trying to tell this young man's fortune," Aladdin scolded. Abu scowled and moved away from the crystal ball.

Aladdin concentrated again. But as hard as he stared, he saw nothing but glass. Time to improvise. Aladdin considered. What kind of fortune would Kalif want to hear? "Kalif, I see wonderful things," Aladdin began. "I see riches beyond compare."

He stole a glance at Kalif. The young man didn't seem very excited.

"I see a huge house with many servants, and a kitchen filled with every kind of food—"

"Yes, yes," Kalif interrupted with a frown. "All that is very nice, but it's not what I want to know about. I want to know the future, not the present."

"The present?" Aladdin asked in surprise.

"Yes. You're telling me what I already know. I have riches and servants, it's true. But I don't care much about those things."

"You don't?" Aladdin and Abu exchanged shocked looks.

Kalif looked wistful. "No. What I want to know is whether I will ever find true love."

Aladdin shrugged. If that's what Kalif wanted to know, fine. And if he was as rich as he claimed, perhaps he would pay more for a favorable fortune. Once again Aladdin looked deep into the crystal ball. "Yes!" he cried. "I see true love in your future!"

Kalif leaned forward, looking interested. "Please, you must tell me about her," he said earnestly. "What will she be like? Tell me so that I will recognize her when I meet her."

"If you insist," Aladdin said. "But that will cost you extra. Three silver pieces."

Kalif waved his hand. "That's no problem. I have plenty of money."

Aladdin considered for a moment. What kind of girl would Kalif fall in love with? Aladdin studied Kalif carefully. Kalif said he had money, but he was dressed modestly. He was tall and heavyset, with dark, serious eyes. His voice was quiet and measured, his words thoughtful, and his expression solemn.

Aladdin gazed again into the crystal ball. "I see the girl!" he cried. "She is wealthy, but not showy. She is tall, and yet not too thin. She has dark, quiet eyes, and she is a thoughtful, serious person." There, that should do it, Aladdin decided. Then he thought of one more thing. "Oh, yes, and she is *very* generous." He held out his hand.

Kalif looked pleased. He nodded in satisfaction. "Now I will surely recognize my one true love when I meet her," he said solemnly. He counted out three silver coins into Aladdin's hand. Then he added an extra one. "Thank you. You've been most helpful. Perhaps I'll come see you again. I may have more questions about this woman."

As Kalif walked away, Aladdin looked down at the money in his hand and grinned. Abu scampered up onto his shoulder to look, too. "Abu, we eat well tonight!" Aladdin said.

Abu rubbed his hands together gleefully. Then he turned a somersault and chattered happily.

"Pomegranates and sugared dates and poppy-seed cake," Aladdin said, licking his lips eagerly. "Maybe this is my own fortune coming true, Abu. Abdullah said I'd be rich someday."

At that moment a young woman hurried up to Aladdin. "Excuse me," she said in a lilting, musical voice. "Are you the fortune-teller?"

"Yes, I am," Aladdin said. He straightened his turban and tried to adopt the serious expression of a professional fortune-teller.

The young woman smiled, displaying dimples in both cheeks. She was petite and very pretty and was dressed in threadbare but colorful clothes. Silver chains decorated with tiny tinkling silver bells adorned her wrists, ankles, and neck. "I would like to have my fortune told, but I don't have very much money." She opened her hand and showed Aladdin a single copper coin. "I've never had much luck with money," she said with a shrug and another smile. "I suppose it runs in my family. Whenever my parents make a little money at their restaurant, they manage to spend every bit." She looked at Aladdin hopefully. "But today they gave me this. Is it enough?"

"Please sit down," Aladdin said, feeling generous. "It so happens that my last customer payed me extra, so I can certainly tell your fortune for a reduced rate."

The young woman sat down. "How sweet of you. My name is Alia. But I suppose, being a fortune-teller, you already knew that."

"Yes," Aladdin said solemnly. "Of course I did. What would you like to learn about your future, Alia?"

Alia giggled and blushed. "Oh, the usual thing."

Aladdin nodded. "I see. You'd like to know if you will become rich."

"No, silly," Alia said. "I want to know when I will meet my one true love."

"Oh, that," Aladdin said. Abu shrugged and looked puzzled.

Aladdin looked deep into the crystal ball. "I see your future now, Alia," he said. "You'll meet your one true love very soon. And . . . and he will be thin, like you." He smiled to himself. This was easier than he'd thought it would be. "Yes, he will be thin, and not too tall. And he will also be happy and friendly and cheerful, like you."

Alia looked thoughtful. Then she smiled widely. "That sounds wonderful. That sounds like just the sort of man I would like. Here is your fee." She handed the coin to Aladdin. "Perhaps if I have more money tomorrow, I will return and you can tell me more."

She gave a little wave as she left, causing her bracelets to tinkle softly. When she had disappeared from sight, Aladdin quickly packed up Abdullah's equipment. All this fortune-telling had made him hungry.

The next day a very well-fed Abu helped a very well-fed Aladdin prepare for another day of business. As they were setting up, Alia rushed up to them. Today she was wearing a dress that was even more brightly colored than the one she'd worn the day before.

"Good morning, fortune-teller," she said cheerfully. "Isn't it a beautiful day?"

"Yes, it is," Aladdin said. "I foresaw that it would be."

Alia held up two shiny copper coins. "My parents had a good day of business at the restaurant yesterday, so they gave me some more money. I wish to hear more of my true love."

"Always at your service," Aladdin said as Abu scampered over with the cushion for her to sit on.

Just then Kalif walked up, looking as somber and serious as ever. "Ah, fortune-teller," he said. "I wanted to get some more details from you on this woman I will meet."

"Certainly, Kalif," Aladdin said. "But first I must help Alia here, if you don't mind waiting."

"Not at all," Kalif said. "I would be happy to wait while such a lovely lady is being helped." He bowed low to Alia.

Alia blushed and giggled. "No, no, please go ahead, kind sir." She smiled up at Kalif, her dimples showing. Side by side they made an odd pair, Aladdin thought. Kalif towered over the delicate Alia, his solemn expression a sharp contrast to her charming smile.

For several moments neither of Aladdin's customers spoke. Aladdin was growing impatient. He wished one of them would just sit down so he could get down to business.

Then it dawned on him that Kalif and Alia were both acting very strangely. They were staring deep into each other's eyes. They seemed to have forgotten all about Aladdin.

"Maybe we could put off having our fortunes told," Kalif suggested at last. "Would you join me for some breakfast, Alia?"

"I'd be delighted," Alia said. "Let's go to my parents' restaurant. I know they'd love to meet you."

To Aladdin's amazement the two of them walked off hand in hand, gazing soulfully into each other's eyes. Aladdin watched

them go. "What just happened here, Abu?" he asked.

Abu shrugged and lifted his fez to scratch his head.

"Ah, my young friend Aladdin. I see all is well."

Aladdin turned around to see Abdullah coming toward the tent. "Abdullah!" Aladdin cried. "You're back! Did you escape from jail?"

"No, the Sultan let me go. He is a very wise ruler. Besides, I told his fortune for him and let him know that he would soon have the perfect suitor for his daughter, the princess." Abdullah shrugged. "I had a feeling I'd be free before long."

Aladdin couldn't help being a little disappointed. He had hoped his fortune-telling career would last longer. Still, he was glad that Abdullah was free again.

Suddenly a question occurred to him. "But how could you tell the Sultan's future without your crystal ball?"

Abdullah pulled a smaller crystal ball from beneath his robe. "I always carry a spare. And you, Aladdin—how did you enjoy being a fortune-teller?"

"It's confusing," Aladdin confessed. "I only had two customers, a man and a woman. I told their futures, and it turned out I was completely wrong in both cases."

"Perhaps you don't have my gift for seeing the future," Abdullah said.

"I guess not. They each wanted to know about the man or woman of their dreams, so I tried to guess. I told Kalif he would fall in love with a woman just like him. And I told Alia she would fall in love with a man just like her."

Abdullah laughed. "It's not always that simple, my young friend."

"I thought that's how love worked," Aladdin said. "I thought people who fall in love with each other usually have a lot in

common."

"Sometimes it works that way, and sometimes not," Abdullah said. "For example, when the Sultan asked me about this suitor for his daughter, the boy I saw for her was very different from the princess."

"Different how?" Aladdin asked.

"Oh, I predict the boy who will win Princess Jasmine's heart is not at all what she—or her father—expects." Abdullah shrugged. "The image was not entirely clear, but I could see that this mysterious boy cares more about money and adventure at the moment than he does about love."

Aladdin grinned and handed the crystal ball back to Abdullah. "Whoever this boy is, I agree with him."

"Yes," Abdullah said, nodding thoughtfully. "I had a feeling you might say that."

A Whole New World

Before the first gray light of dawn, Jasmine bid Rajah good-bye and climbed over the palace wall beyond the menagerie. For the first time, her feet touched ground outside the palace. She looked around quickly, afraid that one of the guards might see her. But all was quiet. A maze of narrow streets confronted her, one much like the next. Which one should she choose?

She spied a donkey drawing a cart. The cart was piled high with melons, and in the front sat a very large, sleepy-looking man. The donkey turned down one of the streets.

"I'll bet he's going to the marketplace," Jasmine said, falling into step behind the cart.

She watched, mesmerized, as the streets slowly came to life around her. Here and there a light flickered in a window. The black of night had given way to a pearly gray, and looking back over her shoulder at the palace that had been her whole world until this day, Jasmine could see the first rays of copper sun strike the peaks of the golden domes.

The street began to fill with people, some shuffling sleepily,

some carrying mountains of goods for the marketplace. Jasmine gazed in fascination at bolts of cloth, baskets of bread, cartloads of brass pots and pans. And there were animals, too—stately camels, a bleating herd of sheep kept in line by a pair of intelligent, watchful dogs, even an ostrich being led on a rope.

As Jasmine hurried along, the city grew brighter, busier, louder. Friends called out to each other. A flute played an intricate tune. Cart wheels clattered on the stones. Donkeys brayed and were answered by the harsh voices of camels.

The sun was already searing by the time Jasmine entered the marketplace, now bustling with the activity of merchants setting out their wares, preparing for the long day ahead. Jasmine twirled around in sheer happiness. She had done it! She had escaped from the palace and the endless stream of awful suitors. She was out in the great wide world with all its wonders.

She gazed at the sights around her. It was even more marvelous than the minimarketplace her father had created in the palace gardens for her birthday a few years back, because this time it was real. Vendors offered to sell her everything from brass pots to sugared dates to fresh fish. Not looking where she was going as she tried to take it all in, she bumped into a fire breather, causing him to swallow his flaming wand. She apologized profusely as he burped up puffs of smoke.

When she turned from him, Jasmine spotted a tattered little boy gazing desperately at a pile of apples. She smiled at him. "Oh, you must be hungry," she said. She chose the shiniest apple and handed it to the boy. "Here you go." The child grinned in astonishment and ran off, clutching his prize.

"You'd better be able to pay for that!" a vendor growled from behind Jasmine.

"Pay?" What exactly did he mean by that? Oh yes, money. Of course, out in the real world people needed money. She'd read about it in a book. "I'm sorry, sir, I don't have any money."

"Thief!" the vendor shouted, looking extremely threatening.

For the first time since her escape, Jasmine began to feel frightened. "Please," she stammered, "if—if you let me go to the palace, I can get some from the Sultan—"

To Jasmine's amazement the vendor whipped out a long, very sharp-looking knife. Then he grabbed Jasmine's arm and pinned it to the counter of his stall. "Do you know what the penalty is for stealing?"

Aladdin had not slept very well. He'd been hungry, yes, but even more, he'd been kept awake by the strangest feeling that something . . . something incredible . . . was about to happen.

But when morning came, the only incredible thing was how easily he and Abu had managed to steal a melon. Atop a merchant's awning Aladdin broke the melon in half and handed Abu his share. "Breakfast is served," he said.

Abu began hungrily devouring his half of the melon. But before Aladdin could take a bite, something caught his eye. He turned and stared in amazement. Walking through the marketplace was the most beautiful girl he had ever seen—more beautiful than anyone he could ever have imagined, with silken black hair, and eyes . . . eyes that could make you forget where you were, or who, or . . .

Abu frowned. Aladdin was suddenly looking very strange—almost as if he'd been put into a trance. Abu jumped onto Aladdin's head and waved a hand in front of his eyes, but Aladdin just kept staring, eyes wide, mouth hanging open.

Suddenly Aladdin jerked back. Abu followed the direction of his gaze and saw a girl. Her hand was being gripped by an angry vendor holding a very sharp knife.

In a flash Aladdin was at her side, just in time to grab the vendor's arm as he brought the knife down. "Thank you, kind sir, I'm so glad you found her," he said quickly. Turning to the

91

girl, Aladdin added, "I've been looking all over for you!" Then he leaned close, so close that he could smell her intoxicating perfume. "Just play along," he whispered.

The vendor grabbed Aladdin. "You know this girl?"

"Sadly, yes, she is my sister," Aladdin answered. He gave the vendor a meaningful look. "She's a little crazy."

"She said she knew the Sultan."

"She thinks the monkey is the Sultan," Aladdin replied, rolling his eyes.

It took Jasmine only a moment to catch on. Quickly she dropped to her knees and bowed to Abu. "Oh, wise Sultan, how may I serve you?"

Aladdin raised her up. "Now come along, Sis. Time to go see the doctor."

Still playing her part, Jasmine stared goofily at a camel. "Hello, Doctor, how are you?"

"No, no, no, not that one," Aladdin said, drawing Jasmine away from the camel. He gestured to Abu. "Come on, Sultan!"

Abu started to follow. But suddenly the apples and coins he'd just stolen from the vendor's stall tumbled out of his vest.

In the brief instant it took the vendor to realize what was happening, Aladdin, Jasmine, and Abu broke into a run. Behind them they heard the vendor's furious cry: "Come back here, you little thieves!"

They ran until the outraged cries faded behind them. Then Aladdin led Jasmine up the series of rickety ladders that led to his rooftop home.

Jasmine looked around the rooftop in surprise. "Is this where you live?" she asked. It was dirty, and certainly not very luxurious, but she had to admit getting there had been fun. Dodging, climbing, even pole-vaulting across the roofs of Agrabah . . .

"Yep, just me and Abu," Aladdin said. "It's not much, but it's got a great view." He drew back the ragged blanket he'd hung

to keep out the cold night winds, revealing the city below and the palace towering over all. "The palace looks pretty amazing, huh?" he said, gazing at it longingly. "I wonder what it would be like to live there and have servants and valets—"

"Oh, sure." Jasmine sighed. "People who tell you where to go and how to dress."

"That's better than here," Aladdin said, lost in his own thoughts. "You're always scraping for food and ducking the guards—"

Jasmine gazed at the palace. "You're not free to make your own choices," she said softly.

"Sometimes you feel so—"

"You're just—"

They both paused, then at the very same moment they both said the same word: "Trapped."

They turned toward each other, and their eyes met. Perhaps it had just been a coincidence. But to Jasmine, the princess, and Aladdin, the street rat, it felt as if maybe, just maybe, they had found the key to a whole new world of happiness in that instant when they'd looked deep into each other's eyes.